I Really Like Slop!

To Cher—
Friend, Chef, and Trier of New Things

ISBN 978-1-338-34356-4

Text and illustrations copyright © 2015 by Mo Willems. All rights reserved. Published by Scholastic Inc., 557 Broadway, New York, NY 10012, by arrangement with Hyperion Books for Children, an imprint of Disney Book Group. ELEPHANT & PIGGIE is a trademark of The Mo Willems Studio, Inc. SCHOLASTIC and associated logos are trademarks and/or registered trademarks of Scholastic Inc.

12 11 10 9 8 7 6 5 4   19 20 21 22 23

Printed in the U.S.A.   40

First Scholastic printing, September 2018

This book is set in Century/Monotype; Grilled Cheese BTN/Fontbros; Neutraface, Fink, Typography of Coop/House Industries.

SCHOLASTIC INC.

An ELEPHANT & PIGGIE Book

5

9

11

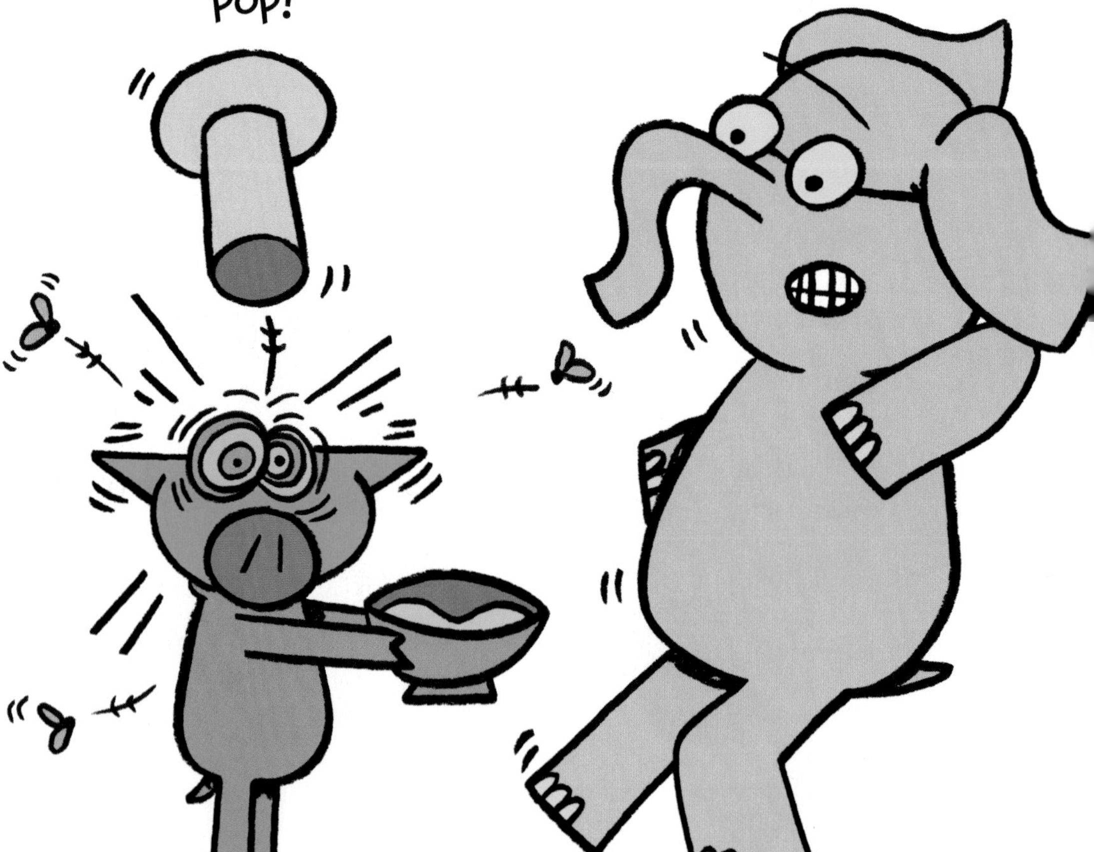
Pop!

27

WALK

Piggie.

I will GULP! try your slop.

40

YOU
TRIED IT!

44

45

46

51

But, I am glad
I tried it.

Have you read all of Elephant and Piggie's funny adventures?